Tiger in the Snow!

Nick Butterworth

Tiger the kitten
has lots of friends.
Usually.
It isn't hard for Tiger
to find someone to
play with. Usually.
But today is an
unusual day.

Snow has covered everything with a chilly white blanket. No one wants to come out to play. Except Tiger.

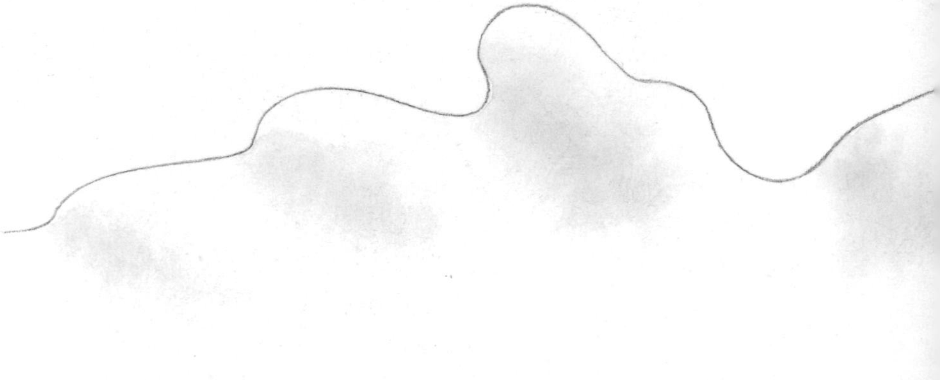

Some are just too busy. For others, it's just too cold...

...and some just won't
come to the door!

Tiger thinks that
perhaps he'll go home.
Then, Tiger sees
something buried
under the snow...

...something unusual.

Tiger pulls the unusual thing out of the snow. He doesn't know what it is...

But Tiger does know
what he wants
it to be...

A sledge!

Tiger thinks it will be great fun to go sliding down a snowy hill.

The sledge agrees
with Tiger and
sets off down the hill
without him!
Tiger races after it
and jumps on.

The sledge goes very quickly. But it doesn't go where Tiger thinks it will go!

Tiger holds tight as the sledge picks up speed.

The sledge seems to be picking up passengers too!

Faster and faster goes the sledge

bouncing and prancing, ever

nd jumping over lumpy bumps...

PULL

nd faster goes the sledge...

Swerving to this side, skidding t

PULL

and straight through the middle

o that side, zigging and zagging, o

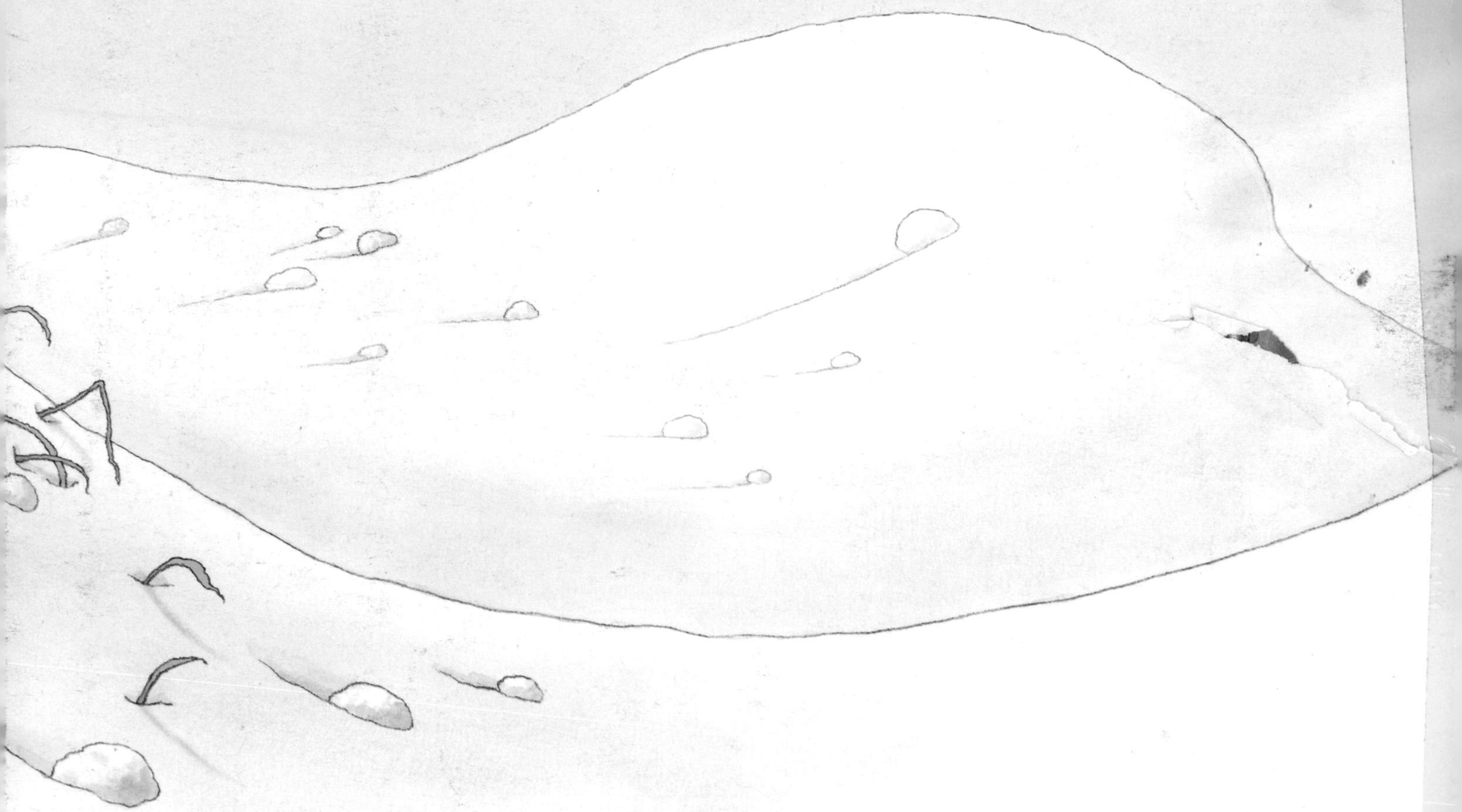

of things... The sledge can't stop. W

ding... bumping over humpy lumps a

g and turning... faster and faster a

slipping and sliding, whizzing and gli

dancing... rocking and rolling, twisti

ver things and under things

won't stop. Doesn't want to stop. And

loesn't stop...

Suddenly,
WHOOOOOOOOSH!
The sledge sails
high into the air...

flying,
spinning,
looping
the loop.
For a
moment,
everything
is quiet.
Then...

FFFLLUMP!

The sledge lands and unloads its

passengers in deep, soft snow.

THAT WAS FUN!

Now, everyone wonders
what to do next...

"LET'S DO IT AGAIN!"
A most unusual day!
as usual!